Chocolates & Candies

Rebecca Gilpin and Catherine Atkinson

Designed and illustrated by Non Taylor

Photographs by Howard Allman

Additional design by Doriana Berkovic

American editor: Carrie Seay   American expert: Barbara Tricinella

Contents

Beside each ingredients list, you can find out how long the chocolates and candies will keep.
If you give them as a present, make sure you also tell the person you are giving them to.
In lots of the recipes, you will use teaspoons and tablespoons for measuring.
Use measuring spoons if you have them, as they give you exactly the amount you need.

Sweethearts

To make about 30 sweethearts, you will need:

¾ cup powdered sugar
¼ cup super-fine granulated sugar
1 cup finely-crushed almonds*
¼ cup full-fat sweetened condensed milk
red food coloring
one medium and one small heart-shaped cookie cutter
a baking sheet covered with wax paper

These candies need to be eaten within four days.

1. Sift the powdered sugar into a large bowl. Add the sugar and almonds and stir them all together.

2. Make a hollow in the middle and add the condensed milk. Mix it in well, until the mixture is completely smooth.

3. Put half of the mixture into another bowl. Add two drops of red food coloring. Mix it in really well, using your fingers.

4. Wrap both pieces of mixture in foodwrap. Put them in a refrigerator for 20 minutes. This makes them easier to roll out.

5. Sprinkle powdered sugar onto a clean work surface. Roll out the pink piece, until it is about as thick as your little finger.

6. Use the larger cutter to cut out heart shapes. Cut them close together. Make the scraps into a ball, and roll it out.

* Don't give these to anyone who is allergic to nuts.

7. Cut out more hearts. Then, use the smaller cutter to cut out hearts from the middles of the big hearts.

8. Roll out the cream mixture, as before. Cut out large hearts. Then, cut small hearts out of their middles.

9. Gently press the small cream hearts into the big pink ones. Then, press the small pink hearts into the big cream ones.

10. Put the hearts onto the baking sheet. Leave them to dry and harden overnight. Store them in an airtight box.

Tropical fruit cups

To make 12 tropical fruit cups, you will need:

2oz. sweetened dried pineapple or mango
1 tablespoon pineapple or orange juice
½ cup milk chocolate or semi-sweet
chocolate chips
½ cup white chocolate chips
small foil or double thickness paper cups
for candy

*These chocolates need to be
eaten within five days.*

1. Put the pineapple or mango onto a cutting board. Using a sharp knife, carefully cut the fruit into tiny pieces.

2. Put about a quarter of the chopped fruit on one side. Put the rest into a small bowl, and add the fruit juice. Stir it well.

3. Cover the bowl with plastic foodwrap. Leave the fruit for half an hour or until it has soaked up the juice.

Do this while the fruit is soaking.

Wear oven gloves when you lift the bowl out.

4. Fill a pan with about 1 in. of water. Heat the pan until the water bubbles, then remove it from the heat.

5. Put the chocolate chips into a heatproof bowl. Wearing oven gloves, carefully put the bowl into the pan.

6. Stir the chocolate with a wooden spoon until it has melted. Lift the bowl out of the pan. Leave it to cool for three minutes.

Spread the chocolate all the way up the sides.

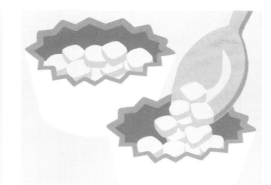

7. Spread chocolate over the inside of the candy cups with a teaspoon. Put them in a refrigerator for 20 minutes, until firm.

8. Spoon some of the soaked fruit into each chocolate cup. Each cup should be just over half full.

9. Melt the white chocolate in the same way that you melted the milk chocolate. Leave it to cool for three minutes.

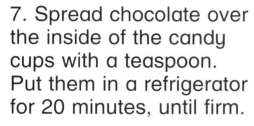

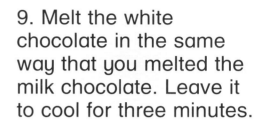

10. Spoon the white chocolate over the fruit, so that it comes right to the top of the milk chocolate cups.

11. Put a piece of fruit on each chocolate. Chill them in a refrigerator for half an hour. Then, peel off the paper cups.

12. Put the chocolates in an airtight container. Keep them in a refrigerator until you are ready to eat them.

Creamy coconut ice

To make 36 squares, you will need:

2 egg whites, mixed from dried or pasteurized
liquid egg white (as directed on package)
1lb. box powdered sugar, sifted
2 cups finely shredded coconut (sweetened)
3 teaspoons water
2 drops green food coloring
a shallow 8in. cake pan
a piece of wax paper

Coconut ice needs to be eaten within 10 days.

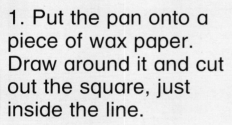

1. Put the pan onto a piece of wax paper. Draw around it and cut out the square, just inside the line.

2. Use a paper towel to wipe some oil onto the sides and bottom of the pan. Press in the paper square and wipe it too.

3. Put the egg whites into a large bowl. Stir them quickly with a fork for about a minute, until they are frothy.

To make pink and white coconut ice, use red food coloring instead of green.

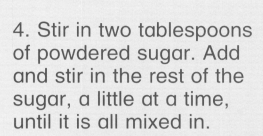 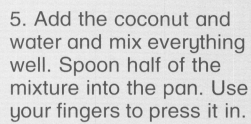

4. Stir in two tablespoons of powdered sugar. Add and stir in the rest of the sugar, a little at a time, until it is all mixed in.

5. Add the coconut and water and mix everything well. Spoon half of the mixture into the pan. Use your fingers to press it in.

6. Add a few drops of green food coloring to the rest of the mixture. Stir the mixture until it is evenly colored.

Smooth the top with the back of a spoon.

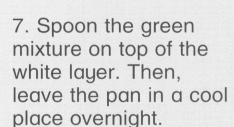

7. Spoon the green mixture on top of the white layer. Then, leave the pan in a cool place overnight.

8. Use a blunt knife to loosen the edges of the coconut ice. Turn it out onto a cutting board. Then, remove the paper.

9. Cut the coconut ice into 36 small squares. Leave them to harden for two hours. Keep them in an airtight container.

Chocolate truffles

To make about 15 truffles, you will need:

1 cup semi-sweet or milk chocolate chips
2 tablespoons butter
¼ cup powdered sugar
¼ cup crushed vanilla wafers
½ cup chocolate sprinkles
paper miniature candy cups

Chocolate truffles need to be eaten within five days.

Put chocolate truffles in boxes lined with tissue paper, to give as presents.

Wear oven gloves when you lift the bowl out.

1. Fill a pan with about 1 in. of water. Heat the pan until the water bubbles, then remove it from the heat.

2. Put the chocolate chips and butter into a heatproof bowl. Wearing oven gloves, gently put the bowl into the pan.

3. Stir the chocolate and butter with a wooden spoon until they have melted. Carefully lift the bowl out of the water.

Use a teaspoon.

4. Sift the powdered sugar into the chocolate. Add the cookie crumbs and stir until everything is mixed well.

5. Leave the chocolate mixture to cool in the bowl. Then, put the chocolate sprinkles onto a plate.

6. When the mixture is firm and thick, scoop up some with a teaspoon and put it into the chocolate sprinkles.

Roll the spoonful to make a ball.

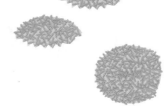

7. Using your fingers, roll the spoonful around until it is covered. Then, put it in a paper cup. Make lots more truffles.

8. Put them onto a plate. Put them in a refrigerator for 30 minutes. Keep them in the refrigerator in an airtight container.

Chocolate-dipped fruit

You will need:

16oz. (1 lb.) small strawberries
   with their stems left on
½ cup milk chocolate chips
½ cup white chocolate chips
a piece of wax paper

The chocolate-dipped fruit needs to be eaten on the day you make it.

You can also dip other kinds of fruit in chocolate. Mandarin orange segments look pretty and taste delicious.

1. Put the strawberries in a sieve. Wash them under cold running water for a little time, to rinse them.

2. Gently pat them with a paper towel to remove most of the water. Then, spread them out on a plate. Leave them to dry.

3. Fill a pan with about 1 in. of water. Heat the pan until the water bubbles, then remove it from the heat.

4. Put the chocolate chips into a heatproof bowl. Wearing oven gloves, carefully put the bowl into the pan.

5. Use a wooden spoon to stir the chocolate until it has melted. Using oven gloves, carefully lift the bowl out of the water.

6. Melt the white chocolate chips in the same way. Leave both bowls of chocolate to cool for two minutes.

7. Dip a strawberry into one of the bowls of chocolate. The chocolate should come about half-way up the strawberry.

8. Lift the strawberry out and let it drip over the bowl. Then, put it on a piece of wax paper on a plate.

9. Dip the other strawberries into the chocolate. Put them in the refrigerator for about 20 minutes, to set.

10. Carefully peel the strawberries off the wax paper, and put them on a plate. Eat them on the same day.

Mini florentines

To make about 18 mini florentines, you will need:

18 Maraschino cherries
18 unsalted mixed whole nuts, such as halved walnuts
  or pecans*
½ cup semi-sweet or milk chocolate chips
½ cup white chocolate chips
a baking sheet covered with wax paper

*Mini florentines
need to be eaten
within four days.*

*These mini
florentines are
topped with
pecan nuts
and cherries.*

1. Put the cherries in a sieve. Rinse them under warm running water to remove the syrup. Dry them on a paper towel.

2. Put the cherries onto a cutting board. Chop each one carefully, using a sharp knife. Then, chop the nuts too.

3. Fill a pan with about 1 in. of water. Heat the pan until the water bubbles, then remove it from the heat.

* Don't give these to anyone who is allergic to nuts.

4. Put the chocolate chips into a heatproof bowl. Wearing oven gloves, carefully put the bowl into the pan.

5. Stir the chocolate with a wooden spoon until it has melted. Using oven gloves, carefully lift the bowl out of the pan.

6. Spoon a teaspoon of melted chocolate onto the wax paper. Make a neat circle, using the back of the spoon.

7. Gently press pieces of cherry and nut into the chocolate. Make more circles of chocolate and decorate them.

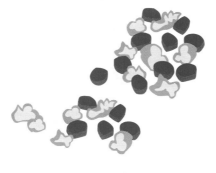

8. Then, melt the white chocolate chips. Make more circles with the chocolate and decorate them too.

9. Put the florentines in the refrigerator for half an hour. Carefully peel them off the paper. Keep them in an airtight container.

Chocolate swirls

To make about 25 chocolate swirls, you will need:

2¼ cups powdered sugar
half the white of a medium egg, mixed from dried or
    pasteurized liquid egg white (as directed on package)
1 teaspoon lemon juice
¼ teaspoon mint extract
1 tablespoon cocoa powder
2 teaspoons boiling water
½ teaspoon vanilla
a baking sheet covered in plastic foodwrap

Eat these within 10 days.

Pour the mixture into the hollow in the powdered sugar.

1. Sift the powdered sugar then put 1 cup of it into a large bowl. Make a hollow in the middle with a spoon.

2. Mix half of the egg white, the lemon juice and mint extract in a small bowl. Pour the mixture into the powdered sugar.

3. Stir the mixture with a blunt knife, then squeeze it with your fingers until it is smooth. Wrap it in plastic foodwrap.

If the mixture is a little dry, add a drop of water.

4. Sift the cocoa powder into a large bowl. Add the water and vanilla. Then, mix everything together well.

5. Add the rest of the egg white and stir it in. Add 1 cup of the powdered sugar. Then, stir the mixture with a blunt knife.

6. Squeeze the mixture until it is smooth. Wrap it in foodwrap. Put both pieces in a refrigerator for 10 minutes.

7. Sprinkle a little of the powdered sugar onto a clean work surface and a rolling pin. This keeps the mixture from sticking.

8. Roll out the white piece of mixture into a rectangle 6 in. by 8 in. Then, do the same with the chocolate mixture.

9. Put the chocolate rectangle on top of the white one. Then, trim the edges with a knife to make them straight.

Roll the rectangle from one of the long edges.

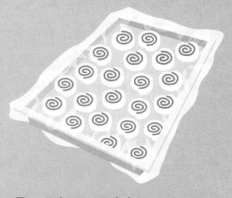

10. Tightly roll the rectangle into a sausage. Wrap it in foodwrap and put it in a refrigerator for about 10 minutes.

11. Using a sharp knife, carefully cut the sausage into slices which are about the thickness of your little finger.

12. Put the swirls onto the baking sheet. Leave them to harden overnight. Keep them in an airtight container.

Chocolate bugs

To make 10 bugs, you will need:

½ cup semi-sweet or milk chocolate chips
3 tablespoons corn syrup
½ cup white chocolate chips

The bugs need to be eaten within a week.

Use a wooden spoon.

1. Fill a pan with about 1 in. of water. Heat the pan until the water bubbles, then remove the pan from the heat.

2. Put the chocolate chips into a heatproof bowl. Using oven gloves, carefully put the bowl into the pan.

3. Stir the chocolate until it has melted. Wearing oven gloves, lift the bowl out of the pan. Leave it to cool for two minutes.

4. Stir in 1½ tablespoons of corn syrup until the mixture forms a thick paste which doesn't stick to the sides of the bowl.

5. Wrap the paste in plastic foodwrap. Then, melt the white chocolate and stir in the rest of the corn syrup, as before.

6. Wrap the white paste in plastic foodwrap. Chill both pieces of chocolate paste in the refrigerator for about an hour.

You could also decorate the bugs with stripes or wiggly lines.

7. Take both pieces of chocolate paste out of the refrigerator. Leave them for about 10 minutes, to soften a little.

8. Cut the chocolate paste into six pieces. Wrap one piece in foodwrap again and put it on one side.

Smooth the edges of the oval shapes.

9. Make the other five pieces into oval shapes. Do the same with the white chocolate paste, to make 10 ovals altogether.

Make a shallow mark with the knife.

10. To make a bug's head, gently press in the back of a blunt knife, a third of the way down a chocolate shape.

The second mark makes the wings.

11. Make a second mark. Unwrap the last pieces of paste. Roll small balls to make eyes and spots. Press them onto the bug.

12. Put the bugs onto a plate. Cover them with plastic foodwrap. Keep them in the refrigerator until you eat them.

Marshmallow crunch

To make about 50 squares, you will need:

1oz. (about 8) candied cherries
2 cups puffed rice cereal
1½ cups miniature marshmallows
2 tablespoons butter
a shallow 8in. cake pan
a piece of wax paper

Marshmallow crunch needs
to be eaten within three days.

1. Put the pan onto a piece of wax paper. Draw around it and cut out the square, just inside the line.

2. Use a paper towel to wipe some oil onto the sides and bottom of the pan. Press in the paper square and wipe it too.

3. Put the cherries onto a cutting board. Carefully cut them into small pieces, using a sharp knife.

4. Put the puffed rice cereal and chopped cherries into a bowl. Mix them well with a wooden spoon.

5. Put the miniature marshmallows into a large pan. Then, add the butter, and mix everything together.

6. Gently heat the pan, stirring occasionally with a wooden spoon. Continue until everything has just melted.

Use a wooden spoon.

7. Remove the pan from the heat. Add the cereal mixture to the pan and stir everything until it is mixed together.

Push the mixture into the corners and smooth it down.

8. Spoon the mixture into the pan, and put it in the refrigerator for two hours. Then, loosen the edges with a blunt knife.

9. Turn the crunch out onto a board. Remove the paper. Cut the crunch into squares. Keep it in an airtight container.

Peppermint creams

To make about 40 peppermint creams, you will need:

2 cups powdered sugar
half the white of a small egg, mixed from dried or
    pasteurized liquid egg white (as directed on package)
¼ teaspoon peppermint flavoring
2 teaspoons lemon juice
red and green food coloring
small cookie cutters
a cookie sheet covered
    in plastic foodwrap

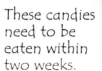

These candies
need to be
eaten within
two weeks.

1. Sift the powdered sugar through a sieve into a large bowl. Make a hole in the middle of the sugar with a spoon.

2. Mix the egg white, peppermint flavoring and lemon juice in a small bowl. Pour the mixture into the sugar.

3. Use a blunt knife to stir the mixture. Squeeze it between your fingers until it is smooth. Then, cut it into two halves.

4. Put each half into a separate bowl. Add a few drops of red food coloring to one bowl, and green coloring to the other.

5. Mix in the red coloring with your fingers. Add more powdered sugar if the mixture is sticky. Mix in the green coloring too.

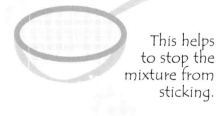

This helps to stop the mixture from sticking.

6. Sprinkle a little powdered sugar onto a clean work surface. Sprinkle some onto a rolling pin too.

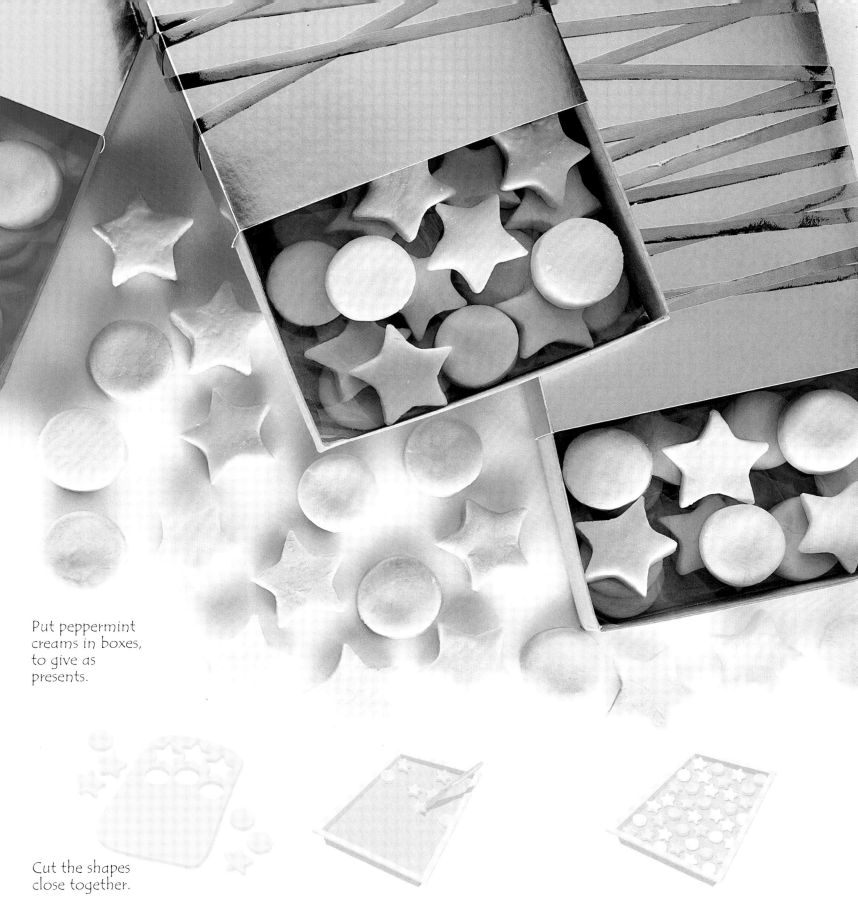

Put peppermint creams in boxes, to give as presents.

Cut the shapes close together.

7. Roll out the pink mixture until it is about as thick as your little finger. Use cutters to cut out lots of shapes.

8. Use a blunt knife to lift the shapes onto a cookie sheet. Roll out the green mixture and cut out more shapes.

9. Put the shapes onto the cookie sheet. Leave them for at least an hour to harden. Keep them in an airtight container.

Orange and lemon creams

To make about 24 orange and lemon creams, you will need:

3½ cups powdered sugar
1 orange (small)
half the white of a small egg, mixed from dried
   or pasteurized liquid egg white (as directed
   on package)
red and yellow food coloring
1 lemon
a baking sheet covered with wax paper

These candies need to
be eaten within 10 days.

Gift bags filled with
orange and lemon creams
make great gifts. Find out
how to make them on
page 30.

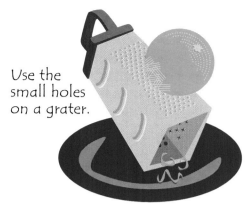

Use the small holes on a grater.

1. Sift the powdered sugar. Put half of it into one bowl and half into another. Grate about half of the skin of the orange.

Use a lemon squeezer.

2. Cut the orange in half and squeeze. Put the juice into a bowl. Then, put 1½ teaspoons of egg white into another bowl.

3. Add the grated orange, 5 teaspoons of juice, a drop of red food coloring and two drops of yellow. Mix everything well.

Add more powdered sugar if it's too moist.

4. Add the mixture to one of the bowls of powdered sugar. Stir it with a blunt knife, then squeeze it with your fingers.

The marks make the outsides look like orange skin.

5. Sprinkle powdered sugar on a clean work surface. Make 12 orange balls. Then, gently roll them over a fine grater.

6. Grate about half of the lemon's skin. Cut the lemon in half. Squeeze it and put 5 teaspoons of the juice into a bowl.

7. Add a few drops of yellow food coloring, the grated lemon and 1½ teaspoons of egg white. Mix everything together.

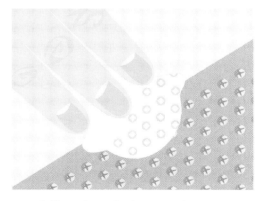

8. Mix the juice mixture into the other bowl of powdered sugar. Make 12 lemon shapes. Roll them over a fine grater.

9. Put the candy onto the baking sheet. Leave them for a few hours to become firm. Keep them in an airtight container.

White marshmallow fudge

To make 36 pieces, you will need:

1lb. box powdered sugar, preferably unrefined
4oz. (about 16) jumbo-sized white marshmallows
2 tablespoons milk
1 stick (½ cup) unsalted butter
½ teaspoon vanilla
a shallow 8in. cake pan
a piece of wax paper

The fudge needs to be eaten within a week.

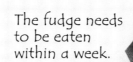

1. Put the pan onto a piece of wax paper. Draw around it and cut out the square, just inside the line.

2. Use a paper towel to wipe some oil onto the sides and bottom of the pan. Press in the paper square and wipe it too.

3. Sift the powdered sugar into a large bowl. Make a small hollow in the middle of the powdered sugar.

4. Using scissors, cut the marshmallows in half and put them into a small pan. Add the milk, butter and vanilla.

5. Gently heat the mixture. Stir it every now and then with a wooden spoon until everything has melted.

6. Pour the mixture into the hollow in the powdered sugar. Beat everything together with a spoon until it is smooth.

Smooth the fudge with the back of a spoon.

7. Put the fudge into the pan and push it into the corners. Use a spoon to make the top of the fudge as flat as you can.

Find out how to wrap pieces of fudge like this on page 31.

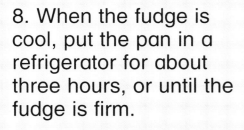

8. When the fudge is cool, put the pan in a refrigerator for about three hours, or until the fudge is firm.

9. Use a blunt knife to loosen the edges of the fudge, then turn it out onto a cutting board. Remove the paper.

10. Cut the fudge into 36 pieces. Then, put it in a refrigerator for an hour to harden. Keep it in an airtight container.

Chocolate and apricot drops

To make about 25 chocolate and apricot drops, you will need:

1¼ cups animal cookies (crumbled)
2oz. (14 halves) dried apricots
1⅓ cups white chocolate chips
4 tablespoons corn syrup
1 teaspoon hot cocoa mix
small paper cups for candy

These chocolates need to be eaten within three days.

1. Break the cookies into tiny pieces and put them into a bowl. Cut the apricots into tiny pieces. Add them to the cookies.

2. Fill a pan with about 1 in. of water. Heat the pan until the water bubbles, then remove it from the heat.

3. Put the white chocolate chips into a heatproof bowl. Wearing oven gloves, carefully put the bowl into the pan.

Wear oven gloves when you lift the bowl out.

4. Stir the chocolate until it has melted. Carefully lift the bowl out of the water. Let the chocolate cool for a minute.

You can also make these chocolates with semi-sweet or milk chocolate, and dust them with powdered sugar.

5. Quickly stir in the corn syrup, then add the cookies and apricots. Mix everything well with a wooden spoon.

6. Scoop up some of the mixture with a teaspoon. Using your hands, shape it into a ball and put it into a paper cup.

7. Make more balls and put them onto a large plate. Put them in the refrigerator for an hour, until they are firm.

8. Sift the cocoa mix over the chocolate and apricot drops. Keep them in an airtight container in the refrigerator.

Chocolate fudge

To make about 36 squares, you will need:

½ cup full-fat cream cheese
2 cups powdered sugar
1 level tablespoon cocoa powder
½ cup semi-sweet chocolate chips
2 tablespoons butter
a piece of wax paper
a shallow 8 in. cake pan

The fudge needs to be eaten within a week.

Find out how to make pointed gift bags on page 30.

Use a pencil to draw around the pan.

1. Put the pan onto a sheet of wax paper. Draw around it and cut out the square, just inside the line.

2. Use a paper towel to wipe some oil onto the sides and bottom of the pan. Press in the paper square and wipe it too.

3. Put the cream cheese into a bowl. Sift the powdered sugar and cocoa into the bowl too. Mix them together well.

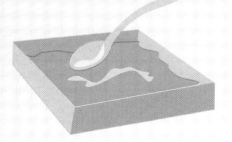

4. Melt the chocolate and butter as in steps 1-3 on page 9. Stir in a tablespoon of the cream cheese mixture.

5. Then, pour the chocolate into the cheese mixture. Beat them together with a spoon until they are creamy.

6. Spoon the mixture into the pan, and push it into the corners. You may need to use your fingers to do this.

7. Smooth the top of the fudge with the back of a spoon. Put the pan in a refrigerator for two hours, or until the fudge is firm.

8. Use a blunt knife to loosen the edges of the fudge, then turn it out onto a cutting board. Remove the paper.

9. Cut the fudge into 36 squares. Put it in a refrigerator for two hours. Keep it in the refrigerator in an airtight container.

Wrapping ideas

Gift bags

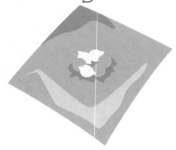

1. Cut a square of thin cellophane. Then, lay five or six pieces of candy in the middle of the square.

2. Gather up the edges of the square around the candy. Then, pull the edges together above the candy, like this.

3. Cut a piece of ribbon about 8 inches long. Tie the ribbon tightly around the bag, above the candy.

Pointed bags

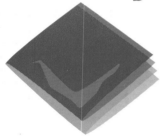

1. Cut a square of cellophane with sides 16 inches long. Fold it in half, and then in half again.

The white line shows you where to cut.

2. Hold the corner where the folds join. Cut a quarter-circle, like this. Open out the cellophane shape. It is now a circle.

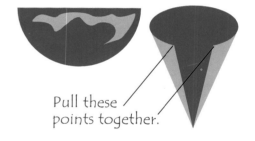

Pull these points together.

3. Cut the circle in half. Take one of the halves. Then, pull its two points towards each other until they meet.

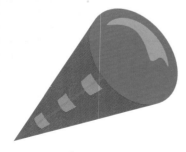

4. Slide one of the points behind the other, to make a cone. Secure the cone with pieces of tape.

5. Half-fill the cone with candy. Cut a piece of ribbon 8 inches long. Tie it around the cone, above the candy.

Line a gift box with cellophane, then fill it with layers of candy.

Wrapped candy

Find out how to make sparkling gift tags on page 32.

Use a tiny piece of tape.

1. Cut a square of thin cellophane that is bigger than the candy. Put the candy in the middle of the square.

2. Wrap the candy in the piece of cellophane and tape it. Tie pieces of ribbon around each end of the candy.

Sparkling gift tags

Ask someone to help you cut the potato.

1. Carefully cut a potato in half. Press the sharp edge of a star-shaped cookie cutter into the cut side of the potato.

2. Press the edge of the star cutter into some household glue. Press the cutter onto a piece of thin cardboard.

3. Before the glue dries, sprinkle it with lots of glitter. Shake off any extra glitter onto some scrap paper.

4. Cut around the star, a little way away from the glitter. Tape a piece of ribbon to the back of the tag.

First published in 2002 by Usborne Publishing Ltd. Usborne House, 83-85 Saffron Hill, London EC1N 8RT, England. www.usborne.com
Copyright © 2002 Usborne Publishing Ltd. The name Usborne and the devices ⊕ ⊕ are Trade Marks of Usborne Publishing Ltd. All rights reserved.
No part of this publication may be reproduced, stored in a retrieval system, or transmitted in any form or by any means electronic,
mechanical, photocopying, recording or otherwise, without prior permission of the publisher. AE First published in America 2002. Printed in Spain.